TICKLE MONSTER

by Josie Bissett

illustrated by Kevan J. Atteberry

COMPENDIUM
kids
inspiring possibilities

The best sound in the world is the glorious sound of my children laughing. Children love playfulness. They love silliness and they LOVE being tickled! Laughing together creates a bond like no other. To me, there is no greater gift than the gift of shared laughter and memories. I thank each and every one of you for giving your child the magical gift of laughter and connection through this book. –Josie Bissett

To **Compendium**, this book would not exist without the collaborative effort from the most creative and inspiring team of people on the planet. Thank you, thank you! To **Kobi Yamada**, once again, thank you for your faith in me. I marvel at your ability to run an amazing company that inspires the world while keeping the rest of your life in balance. I cherish our friendship. To **Dan Zadra**, for your remarkable way with words. I thank you deeply for your dedication, heart and spirit on this project. Your calm, steady nature makes working together heavenly. To **Kevan Atteberry**, super illustrator. Thank you sooooooooooo much for bringing my furry friend to life. To **Jessica Phoenix** and **Sarah Forster**, a huge thank you for your art direction, attention to detail and your dedication to refining this book. To **Kristel Wills**, a special coffee drinkin' toast—you rock. Thanks for taking the bull by the horns and gettin' the Tickle Monster party started. To **Heidi Wills**, for all your creative and thoughtful ideas. You are my kinda girl. You do what you do with oodles of grace, big wide eyes and a sparkling smile. To **Nancy Iannios**, my incredible publicist, for your dedication to making my projects shine. Thank you so much to **Gina Coheley**. Yikes! What would I do without you?! Thanks for keepin' things in order. You're the best. To **Rob Estes**, thank you for being you and keeping the kids laughing. Your ability to juggle and be wholly present in your passions and fatherhood always amazes me. To **my family**, I am especially grateful for your love and never ending support. Thank you, I love you all. To my **dad** and **mom**, a super duper special thanks for always believing in me, allowing me to follow my dreams and for enduring my "inappropriate" bouts of laughter. To **Jenny Gibbs**, **Janice Pope**, **Mary Goodman**, **Suzy McQuaid**, **Karen Rauber**, **Rayne Nahajski**, **MJ Sander**, **GG Jacobs**, **Robyn Armani**, **Michelle Peecock**, **Vanessa Fiola** and **Gillian Whitlock**. You are my treasured soul sisters. Oh, how I wish there was more time in the day to just play like little girls! I am eternally grateful for all your love and support, the shared laughter and tears, and endless powwows about life. To **Jeff Reed**, with love, appreciation and enormous gratitude. You keep me grounded—I couldn't have done it without you. I love your kind, generous and gentle nature. You are so good to me and I thank you for everything. To my little angels **Mason** and **Maya**, from the depths of my soul, thank you for blessing me with your contagious ever-present laughter. And a gi-normous thanks for letting me "test" my tickles on your bellies.

When I think of all the blessings in my life, I think of each and every one of you.

With love and gratitude, Josie

CREDITS

Written by Josie Bissett
Illustrated by Kevan J. Atteberry
Edited by Dan Zadra & Kristel Wills
Designed by Jessica Phoenix & Sarah Forster

Library of Congress Control Number: 2008924366

ISBN: 978-1-932319-67-5

Text copyright © 2008 by Josie Bissett
Illustrations copyright © 2008 by Kevan J. Atteberry

All rights reserved. No part of this publication may be reproduced or transmitted in any form or by any means, electronic or mechanical, including photocopy, recording, or any storage and retrieval system now known or to be invented without written permission from the publisher. Contact: Compendium, Inc., 600 North 36th Street, Suite 400, Seattle, WA 98103. Tickle Monster, Compendium, live inspired and the format, design, layout and coloring used in this book are trademarks and/or trade dress of Compendium, Incorporated. This book may be ordered directly from the publisher, but please try your local bookstore first. Call us at 800-91-IDEAS or come see our full line of inspiring products at www.live-inspired.com.

Printed in China with soy-based inks. A021107010030

Dedicated to Mason and Maya,
my little Tickle Monsters

I come from **Planet Tickle**, you see,

I'm a monster, but not the kind you must flee.

I'm the happiest, silliest, zaniest kind.

My talent is TiCKLiNG,

I think you'll soon find.

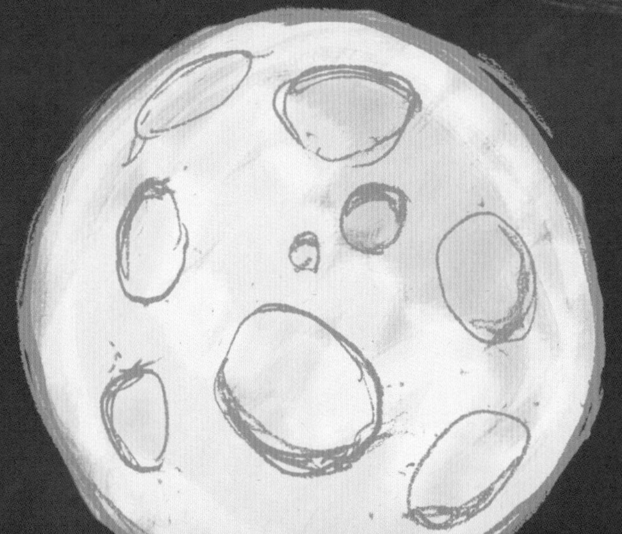

I've traveled the galaxy, planets and stars.
I've TICKLED my way from Venus to Mars.
I've traveled the world from Texas to Pisa.
I've TICKLED King Tut and the Great Sphinx at Giza.

TiCKLiNG my lovies is what I do **best.**

Are you sure you're ready for what's coming next?

I'm all in a tizzy, quite frizzy and dizzy,
My fingers are squiggly, your piggies are wiggly.

I may not be right, but I'd venture to say

You ought to be **TiCKLeD** ten times a day.

So please don't you move, you better stay putsie,

My first stop will be **your**...

...adorable footsie!

I need just a moment, as a matter of factly,
To scheme where I'll TiCKLe you next exactly.
I'll tell you a secret, you sweet little pea,
It's time to TiCKLe your...

...cute boney knee!

I want you to know the TiCKLes are ending
(Not true, of course, I'm only pretending).
Get ready for **laughter**, cuz here I come
To **TiCKLe** and tackle your...

...little tum-tum!

Let's stop if you will, I have a request.
My fingers are tired, they need a short rest.
Just for a moment, let's make funny faces
Be fishes or monkeys or something OUTRAGEOUS.

Surely, by now, you must be believing
My space ship is waiting and soon will be leaving.
So let's say good-bye—oh, my, what the heck—
I've decided to stay and NIBBLE your...

...neck!

No camel or kitten, or bulldog or beagle,
No kangaroo, elephant, zebra or eagle,
No octopus, platypus, chipmunk or toucan,
Knows how to **giggle** as well as you can.

With big mitts like mine, my talents are obvious.
Everyone says my **TiCKLiNG** is marvelous.
Here let me prove it—holy moly kind kitties—
The next place to **TiCKLe** is your...

...underarm-pitties!

Hold still, now—no jumping, or flinching or wiggling,
No smiling, or smirking, or **snorting** or **giggling**.

Now comes the moment for us to be serious.
Next you shall see something *verrrry* **MySTeRious**.

For my crowning achievement
I'll TiCKLe your toes,

And your elbows, your knees,
your neck and your nose,

And your earlobes, your eyebrows
your chin—quite a tally—

I'll TiCKLe them ALL
for my big GRaNd FiNaLe!

Whew! That's enough, I'm exhausted from **laughing**.
I've had so much fun, what a great time we're having.
But now I must leave—find my coat, grab my hat—
Planet Tickle is calling; it's time for my nap.

Now please don't you worry and please don't you fret,
Because **TICKLE MONSTER** isn't done with you yet.
Here's one more thing before I must go...

...I love YOU so much,
I want you to know!